11376

50 MYSTERIES I CAN SOLVE

Written By Susannah Brin
And Nancy Sundquist
Illustrated By Neal Yamamoto

ISBN 0-8431-1869-5

Mysterious Treasure

Ships have been sailing the seven seas for thousands of years. Over the years many ships were lost at sea. Today, divers and treasure hunters search the bottoms of oceans looking for sunken ships. The deep holds many mysteries waiting to be solved.

Study the picture below. How many hidden treasures can you find in the picture?

The Elevator Mystery

Timmy Thompson lived on the fourteenth floor of a high-rise apartment building. Timmy was six years old and only three feet tall. Everyday, he would leave his apartment on the fourteenth floor and take the elevator to the first floor. When he came home from school, he rode the elevator to the fourth floor. He got off on the fourth floor and then climbed the ten flights of stairs to his apartment.

Why didn't Timmy take the elevator all the way to his apartment?

3

A Whodunit For Super Sleuths!

Rain pounded on the windows of the jailhouse visiting room. Lawyer Lawrence Larousse sat at a table across from his new clients – Huey, Duey and Louey Cheats. Mr. Larousse had defended criminals before, but he had never known such liars as the Cheatses. *The truth was always the opposite of what they said.*

Mr. Larousse lifted a legal pad and his favorite gold fountain pen from his briefcase. "I'm going to have to take *very* careful notes with *this* case," thought Mr. Larousse as he set his paper and pen on the table.

Just then lightning flashed and the room went dark. Just as quickly, the lights came back on. Mr. Larousse stood up in shock. His shiny gold fountain pen was gone!

"All right, you guys," Mr. Larousse said rather angrily. "Which one of you took my pen?"

One by one, the brothers answered.

Huey: "I took it."

Duey: "Huey took it."

Louey: "It wasn't Huey or Duey."

Help Mr. Larousse decide which one of the Cheats brothers took his favorite fountain pen. Here's a hint. The opposite of each man's answer to Mr. Larousse's question is the truth.

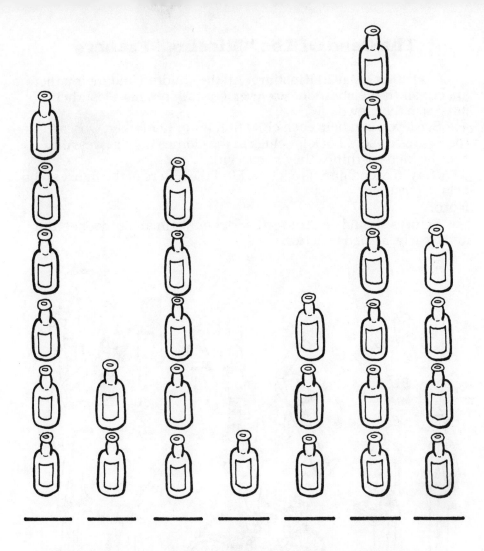

The Mystery Of The Unlabeled Bottles

Old Widow Jones went to the drugstore every day for a week.
At the drugstore she bought bottles of poison to kill the rats that
lived in her barn. What kind of poison did Old Widow Jones buy?
To find out, solve this two-part puzzle.

First count the bottles in each row. Write the number of bottles
in each row on the line below the row. Next, write the letter that
goes with each number you have written above. The letters will
spell the name of the poison.

<u>6</u>   <u>2</u>   <u>5</u>   <u>1</u>   <u>3</u>   <u>7</u>   <u>4</u>

—   —   —   —   —   —   —

6	0	4	0	1	0	0	0	7	0	0	0	0
A	B	C	D	E	F	G	H	I	J	K	L	M

3	0	0	0	2	5	0	0	0	0	0	0	0
N	O	P	Q	R	S	T	U	V	W	X	Y	Z

5

The Case Of The "Missing" Fathers

It's Father's Day in Kinsburg. All the children and their fathers are out for the celebration. However, six children have lost their fathers in the crowd.

See if you can help each child find his or her father. Observe the figures closely. Look for clues in the clothes they're wearing and the kinds of things they're carrying.

Next to each figure is a letter. Find the letters of the figures who belong together.

Note:

Figures should be arranged horizontally in an outdoor setting and clearly labeled by letter.

The Coin Puzzle Mystery

A rare gold coin was stolen from a plate in the museum. Clever Heather, a detective for the Solve-It Detective Agency, was called in to solve the case. First, she learned that Snidely Swipe, a notorious thief, was last seen standing by the table where the coin lay on the plate. No one else went near the table. Clever Heather reasoned that Snidely Swipe had taken the coin, but no fingerprints were found. Clever Heather questioned Snidely Swipe for hours. Finally, he confessed that he had taken the coin, but he had not touched the coin or the plate.

How could Snidely Swipe take a coin out of a plate without touching either?

Coffee Caper

Mysteries are often puzzles that can be solved by clear thinking. Read the following puzzle. Then solve the mystery of the Coffee Caper.

Sam the Sugarman had a sweet tooth. He loved to steal sugar cubes. One day, he hid a cube of sugar in coffee. Later that same day, he retrieved his lump of sugar from the coffee.

How could Sam the Sugarman drop a cube of sugar into coffee without the sugar cube getting wet?

The Tricky Clue

Super Sleuth Sam had been working on a difficult case for a year. He was looking for the famous jewel thief, Diamonds Malone. Diamonds Malone knew that Super Sleuth Sam was looking for him. But Diamonds wasn't worried. In fact, he liked to tease Super Sleuth Sam by sending him little clues.

One day, Diamonds sent Super Sleuth Sam one too many clues. In the note below is the tricky clue Diamonds Malone sent Super Sleuth Sam. Super Sleuth Sam figured out the tricky clue and found where Diamonds Malone was hiding. Super Sleuth recovered the jewels and put Diamonds Malone behind bars.

Read Diamonds Malone's note. Can you figure out where he was living?

Dear Super Sleuth Sam,
Catch me if you can. I know you've been looking for me for a long time so here is a tricky clue. I am living in a square house. Each side of the house faces south.
Your trench coat is going to wear out before you ever find me. Ha, ha, ha.

> **Love,**
> **Diamonds**

Puzzler

Julia Brown had a very special science project for the sixth grade Science Fair. Her project consisted of a bottle of liquid. When asked what the liquid was, Julia explained that she had discovered how to make a liquid that could dissolve all substances.

How do you know that the bottle full of liquid could not dissolve all substances as Julia claimed?

You Be The Eyewitness

You have just witnessed a crime. Later, a police detective asks you to describe the person you saw leaving the scene of the crime. Read the following short description of the person, then wait one minute. After one minute, write your description of the person on a piece of paper. Did the two descriptions match?

Your description:

The Mysterious Dinosaur Drawings

Joey Miller liked to play tricks on his friends. One day, he decided to draw pictures of dinosaurs on the rocks in the old stone canyon. After he finished the drawings, he ran to tell his friends that he had made a great scientific discovery.

"I've made an important scientific discovery," said Joey to his friends.

"What?" asked Bobby suspiciously.

"Old, very old pictures of dinosaurs," said Joey.

Joey's friends followed him to the canyon to look at the dinosaur drawings.

"These drawings were drawn by someone who lived during the age of dinosaurs," said Joey.

All of Joey's friends were very impressed except Bobby.

"These dinosaur drawings may be old," said Bobby, "but they weren't drawn during the age of dinosaurs. In fact, you probably drew these dinosaur pictures to trick us."

How did Bobby know that the dinosaur pictures were not drawn during the time dinosaurs roamed the earth?

Vanished

It had been many years since Jose had seen his hometown of Puerto Bello. He and his family had been forced to leave the beautiful seaside village the year the hurricane destroyed their home – and much of the village as well. The storm had even taken with it much of Puerto Bello's famous beach.

Jose was in a small motor boat, puttering slowly out of the harbor. He was happy to see that Puerto Bello had rebuilt itself. Once again, tourists had returned to the city to enjoy its peaceful air. "No doubt, they are taking home the best of the seashells," thought Jose, a bit unhappily. Seashells were his favorite things. He believed they should be enjoyed, but left where they were found.

Soon Jose was passing Rico Rivera's cement factory, which made a loud grinding noise. Jose looked over his shoulder and watched one of Rivera's steam shovels drop tons of salt-like sand into a chute. Jose had never seen so much sand in his entire life. Briefly, he wondered where Rivera had found it all.

As Jose's boat carried him farther out into the harbor, the noise of the factory slowly faded. Jose was on his way to visit his old favorite spot for seashells. It was one of two tiny islands that were hidden from the harbor by a gigantic rock. He remembered it having the whitest sand he had ever seen.

Finally, Jose reached the wet, black rock. He looked out over the sea, toward the tiny two islands. He could not believe his eyes. His favorite island had vanished, was completely gone! Only the other remained. . . .

What happened to Jose's favorite island? The story gives clues to three possible explanations. What are they and which one makes the most sense?

The Tell-Tale Clock

Minute Marty was the fastest boy in Cooperville. His name wasn't really Minute but people called him that because he tried to do everything in a minute.

Once, Minute Marty solved a mystery in a minute. The day he solved the mystery, he was having a one-minute haircut at Bob's Barber Shop. Now, Bob's Barber Shop was an interesting place because it was divided into two shops. One part of the shop was the barber shop and the other part was Bob's Clock Shop. Minute Marty liked to sit in the barber chair and look at the clocks from the clock shop reflected in the barber's mirror.

While Bob was cutting Minute Marty's hair, the chief of police entered the barber shop.

"Hi. Did you solve any mysteries today?" asked Minute Marty.

"Not yet. But I'm working on one," said the chief. "In fact, I came to ask Bob a few questions. I'm sure you've heard that Banker Smith's house was robbed yesterday."

"Sure did," said Bob the Barber.

"Well, I think I've got a suspect. Widow Miller saw Jimmy Sticky Fingers walking past Banker Smith's house yesterday, about the time the robbery could have happened. She said that Jimmy was walking past the house at about 11:05."

"So what is the problem, Chief?" asked Minute Marty.

"Well, Jimmy says he was having his hair cut here at Bob's at 11:05. He claims that he could see the clock in the mirror and the clock said 11:05. So if he was here, how could Widow Miller see him at Banker Smith's house at 11:05?"

"He was here, Chief. I remember looking at the clock reflected in the mirror and it read 11:05," said Bob the Barber.

"Wait a mighty minute," said Minute Marty, "I think Widow Miller could have seen Jimmy Sticky Fingers at 11:05 because Jimmy wasn't here at 11:05, he was here at 12:55."

How did Minute Marty know that Jimmy Sticky Fingers was not at Bob's Barber Shop at 11:05?

GSV/Y L B H/Z M W
R'OO/Y F H G/B L F
L F G/Z G/H F M W L D M.
Y V/I V Z W B!

The Cherry Pie Connection

All was quiet at Dry Gulch county jail. Sheriff Leadfoot was slumped in his chair and snoring loudly. A fly buzzed around his head and finally settled on Leadfoot's nose.

Suddenly, the door rattled open. Leadfoot's fingers came to life and curled around the gun he wore at his hip. He opened one eye, then the other. Standing before him was none other than Sneaky Pete – the dreaded horse thief, hold-up man, stagecoach robber and card shark!

Sneaky Pete was covered with dirt from some unlawful activity. In one hand, he held a pie, which was in a pretty blue and white box from Marie's Bakery.

Leadfoot guessed that Sneaky Pete was there to see Wild Man Willy, the only prisoner the Dry Gulch jailhouse held. Leadfoot wasted no time. "No visitors allowed," he shouted before Sneaky Pete could say a word.

"There can't be any law against giving a prisoner a cherry pie!" Sneaky Pete growled.

Leadfoot had to admit Sneaky Pete had a point. "Ok, Ok," Leadfoot said. "But it's me who's going to give it to him."

"Just make sure you do, or you'll be hearing from me," said Sneaky Pete. Then he clumped out the same door he entered.

Leadfoot looked hungrily at the pie. "No reason the prisoner should be treated better than the prison keeper," he thought to himself. Carefully, he slid the pie out of the box. Then he took a knife from his pocket and cut out a slice.

The pie was no sooner in Leadfoot's mouth than he had to spit it out. The reason? There was a cherry that wouldn't be chewed! Leadfoot lifted the cherry up with the point of his knife blade and eyed it closely. Suddenly, he realized that it wasn't a cherry at all! It was a rolled up piece of paper!

Leadfoot smoothed out the gooey paper on his desk top. It contained letters that spelled nothing Leadfoot could read. Was this a special code Marie used at her bakery? Or was it a coded message to Wild Man Willy from Sneaky Pete?

Show Leadfoot that the paper indeed contains a message for Wild Man Willy. Decode it for him. Here's a hint: *A = Z* and *Z = A!* Here's how to use the hint: First, write the letters of the alphabet across a sheet of paper, from left to right. Now, beneath this row of letters, write out the alphabet again, this time from *right to left*.

What is the first letter in Sneaky Pete's message? It is the letter *G*. Find the letter *G* in the backwards alphabet. What is the letter above it? It is the letter *T*. Write the letter *T* in the first blank provided above Sneaky Pete's message. Continue decoding the message, letter by letter. When you have filled in all the blanks, you'll be able to read the note to Wild Man Willy easily!

Picture Word Clues

Charley Parker and his father Tom decided to go camping. So they packed the car with their camping equipment and set off for the woods. When they got to the woods, they decided to set up camp near the lake. First, they unpacked the car. Then, they set up their tent. While Charley's father unrolled the sleeping bags inside the tent, Charley wandered off to look for firewood.

While looking for wood, Charley discovered a big cave in the side of the mountain. Since Charley was a very curious person, he decided to explore the cave. At first, he couldn't see anything inside the cave because it was dark. But suddenly, Charley saw something that made his hair stand on end!

What did Charley see?

A Study In Orange

Dr. Dudley Dodd was known throughout Hillsborough as the Sherlock Holmes of medicine. From time to time, people would come down with strange illnesses. Dr. Dodd could often tell them what was wrong simply by asking a few questions.

One of Dr. Dodd's most unusual cases occurred one day in early summer. He entered his office to find the patient, Ramona Rousseau, standing at the window with her back turned toward him. She was wearing a suit and a wide-brimmed hat. At her feet was a large, black leather portfolio – the kind of case that artists use to carry their work.

"Hello," the good doctor said, closing the door behind him. "I'm Doctor Dodd. How may I help you?"

Dr. Dodd immediately noticed that her skin appeared to be a strange shade of orange.

"It's my skin, Doctor," said Ramona with some puzzlement in her voice.

Ramona unzipped her portfolio and spread out nine paintings on the desk. All of them were of shapes painted in various hues of orange.

"Recently, I became interested in the color orange. I began working night and day, studying it in all its shades. Of course, I bathed every day to wash off the paint. I live alone in a small studio. After a month, I realized the paint was in the air and that my skin was absorbing it! But if anything, my skin seems to be growing more orange than ever!

"I see," said Dr. Dodd. "Now tell me, Miss Rousseau, how are you feeling – aside from the natural anxiety over your skin?"

"Well, fine!" said Ramona.

"What about your eating habits? Has there been any change in them recently?"

"Not at all. I'm very careful about what I eat, Doctor. You see, I'm a vegetarian. As a matter of fact, this year I've even grown my own vegetables."

"Take my carrot patch. Every morning, I pick a few and put them in the blender. That gives me at least three glasses of juice a day.

"Then I use some to make carrot cake. Then there's carrot souffle, which is quite good, too."

By the end of Ramona Rousseau's office visit, Dr. Dodd had learned all he needed to know. He knew exactly what had caused Ramona's skin to change color and how to get it back to normal.

What caused Ramona's skin to turn orange, and what do you think Dr. Dodd advised her to do?

Carmelita Cooke And The Seven Crooks

See how good a detective you are and find all the mistakes you can in this story.

Carmelita Cooke was one of the smartest, most successful and most powerful crooks in all of North America. But Carmelita was nothing without her band of seven thieves. They, in turn, were nothing without her. She was the brains behind their operations, and they were the brawn. In other words, they did all the dirty work while Carmelita waited in safety for their return.

Carmelita was also one of the wealthiest crooks around. She spent every penny she stole. She owned many homes throughout the world – all paid for in cold cash. Each was lavishly furnished and maintained by a full staff of servants.

Her headquarters were in Chicago – a beautiful one room studio apartment overlooking Lake Superior. It was here that she held monthly meetings with the seven men. Together, they reviewed their past performance and discussed future plans.

On Thursday, December 30, the gang was gathered around Carmelita's banquet table in her dining room, behind closed doors. The maid had cleared away the luncheon dishes and gone home for the day.

The room was silent, and the men waited for Carmelita to sum up their plans for the next job. Gazing out her window, Carmelita watched the setting sun slip behind the lake. Suddenly, she turned around and leaned her forearms on the table.

"Then it's settled," she said. "We'll break into the museum Sunday, January 1, at 8 P.M. sharp. Lefty, Jake, Fast Eddy and Fingers – the four of you will raid the museum. Fast Eddy, I want you to be the one to take the Picasso paintings. Jake, you stand guard. Possum, you and Billy will wait in the car."

January 1 arrived, and everything went as planned. Yet the adventure was doomed from the start. As soon as Lefty emerged from the museum with the Picasso under his jacket, nine squad cars appeared out of nowhere. Each car held two officers.

As the thieves were being read their rights, so too was Carmelita, back at company headquarters. To this day, no one knows who placed the anonymous call to the police warning them of the museum break-in. And to this day, Carmelita and her seven crooks remain in jail. Their only comfort is in knowing that it took three times their number to shut their business down!

The Case Of The Secret Markings

Once upon a time there was a country called Upper Egomania. It was ruled by King Ferdinand Id III. Now King Ferdinand was the kind of ruler who liked to see his picture everywhere. All citizens were required to hang one in their homes. All street signs carried the smiling face of the king. And needless to say all postage stamps also showed the king – in various poses and royal garbs.

The king ordered the Royal Bureau of Printing and Engraving to issue a new stamp of him every month. Now, the Royal Stamp Artists were not a happy crew. Not only did the king make them work long, hard hours, while paying them poorly. The king also criticized their drawings in front of the other artists and he forbade them to sign their work! Two of the youngest artists, Harlin and Beaufield, were ready to revolt.

"Ferdinand here, Ferdinand there – I'm sick, I tell you, of seeing his face!" whispered Harlin over his drafting table. "*I* would look much better on the stamp."

"I myself think the king's last name is Id because he's an *idiot*!" snorted Beaufield, who was mixing new colors of inks. "I've been thinking about our sorry state of affairs, my friend, and have hit upon an idea. There's a way we can make these stamps ours and ours alone! It will make us feel ever so much better, but no one can know."

"Pray tell. What is it?" asked Harlin hopefully.

Little did Beaufield and Harlin know that many artists before them had tried their little trick. King Ferdinand was ready for them. Before Beaufield's and Harlin's stamps were printed, a Royal Private Eye was employed to inspect them!

Be the Royal Private Eye. Examine the stamps below. What trick did Beaufield and Harlin attempt to play on the king?

Sidetracks #1

Who, or what, left these tracks on the ground?

Faking It

C.C. Malone picked up the crisp, new one hundred dollar bill, or C note. He wasn't known as C.C. for nothing – his money looked like the real thing. C.C. held the bill up to the light to admire his handiwork. Then he looked at his watch. He and his sidekick, "Pockets" Purdue, were running late.

"Hurry up with those ones, will ya?" C.C. yelled.

Pockets was bent over a small printing press in the corner of the room. He was looking at one of their fake one dollar bills with a magnifying glass. "Let me just check one more thing," Pockets replied.

"Forget it," C.C. grumbled. "We don't have time for your nit-picking!" By now C.C. was shoveling stacks of fake one hundred, fifty, twenty, ten and five dollar bills into a suitcase.

One week later, C.C. was wishing he'd let Pockets check out those one dollar bills. For now both men were in jail, where they had all the time anyone could ever want.

Can you find the mistake C.C. and Pockets made? (HINT: You don't need a magnifying glass to spot it. Also, it might help to borrow a real dollar bill and compare the two.)

17

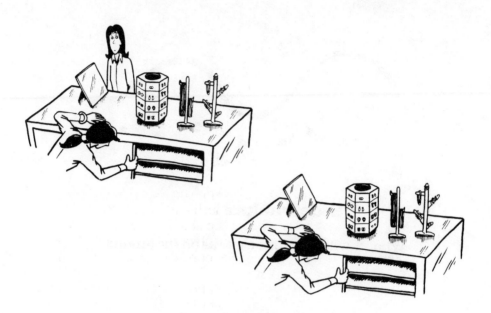

Curtain Call At Lacy's

Lacy's department store was a popular place among shoplifters. They kept the store detective busy. And because they knew him by sight, he appeared for work every day in a new disguise!

One day, Barrymore arrived at Lacy's disguised as a British nobleman – complete with top hat, monocle, cape and cane. He had dyed his black hair blond and wore a blond mustache and small pointy, blond beard called a goatee. Not even the clerks recognized him. Barrymore paused inside the store entrance, then sauntered over to the jewelry department.

"May I help you, sir?" asked Gladys, a clerk who was hoping for a big sale from the wealthy-looking gentleman.

Barrymore held his monacle over one eye and looked down at the glass display case. Out of the corner of his eye, he noted the approach of the notorious shoplifter Molly Sweetwater.

"Why, thank you, my dear," Barrymore said to Gladys – trying to sound very British, of course. "I think I should like to examine that ruby ring on the bottom shelf."

Popping her gum loudly, Molly Sweetwater began looking at necklaces hanging from a post to Barrymore's left. Gladys bent down to reach for the ring. At the same time, Barrymore felt himself being nudged on his right. He turned and saw a young man, who kindly excused himself. Immediately, Barrymore realized the man was in cahoots with Molly! Quickly, Barrymore whipped around. But it was too late. Molly Sweetwater was gone and so too was a piece of jewelry.

All of this happened even before Gladys was able to reach the ruby ring! But Barrymore moved fast too. By the time Molly made her way through the store, Barrymore was outside waiting for her.

But what piece of jewelry did Molly Sweetwater attempt to take? Look at the pictures of the display case before and after Molly left it. What is in the first picture that is not in the second?

The Hunt Is On!

You are a detective. You have been on the trail of an enemy spy by the name of Fraser Caulfield for months. Finally, you are close to catching him in the act of delivering top secret information to a dangerous man who goes by the name George Hunicott. You know that they are planning to get together soon. You want to be there when they do.

You have gained entry into Fraser's hotel room. Immediately, you spot a suspicious-looking note next to the phone. You see that Fraser has started to decode the message, then must have thought better of it:

Try to crack the code. Start by writing out the 26 letters of the alphabet across a sheet of paper. Beneath the letters A-C-L fill in the numbers that Fraser has already identified. See if you can determine the pattern and complete the code for the entire alphabet. Once you do, decoding the secret message will be easy!

Mixed-Up Wanted Posters

Art and Bart are twins. They are also train robbers. The Texas Rangers have been trying to catch Art and Bart for two years. So far Art and Bart have not been captured. From descriptions of Art and Bart, an artist was able to draw a picture of the twin robbers. Art and Bart's faces appear in the wanted poster below.

Can you find Art and Bart among the wanted posters? Remember, Art and Bart are twins, so their pictures must look exactly alike. Look closely at the details in each picture.

The July Meeting Of The Mayfield Women's Mystery Club

The Mayfield Women's Mystery Club had only seven members.
Every month, one of the women hosted a meeting at her home.
She would serve a snack and then present a mystery. The member
who solved it first won a small prize.

In July, it was Mabel Peabody's turn to host. At 6:45, the
members began to arrive. By 7:00 sharp, all were sitting in Mabel's
living room in eager anticipation of the month's mystery.

Mabel stood before the women and announced that the mystery
would begin in the guestroom. However, she went on to say, that
she wished to serve dinner first. Under no circumstance was any
member allowed in the guestroom before dinner. (This was a new
rule that Mabel had added. She had observed at past meetings
certain members trying to get a head start on the others in solving
the mystery.)

Mabel went into the kitchen to check on her popular vegetable
stew. It was doing nicely, but still needed a few more minutes. She
set out seven bowls, and then on a whim decided to check the
guestroom.

There, she was stunned by what she found on the desk. One of
the members had been inside the room snooping around!

**Look at the pictures of the desk in Mabel's guestroom and
of the mystery club members in her living room. Can you guess
which one sneaked into the guestroom?**

Trapped!

Fredrika Forsythe stood in line at Kennedy Airport in New York City. She and the other passengers in line had just arrived from Europe. Everyone's baggage would be searched before being allowed to enter the United States.

"What's taking them so long?" Fredrika muttered under her breath, to no one in particular.

But the gentleman standing in front of her heard her complaint. With his hand over his mouth, he leaned back toward Fredrika and whispered, "I hear there was a spy on our flight – someone claiming to be a citizen of the United States. They're checking all the women very closely."

"I see," replied Fredrika, tucking her briefcase tightly under one arm. She watched the airport guard at the head of the line. He was indeed asking the woman standing before him an unusual number of questions.

Quickly, Fredrika's eyes darted from the guard to the exit door and to the police on either side. Then she noticed the women's restroom on her right.

"Excuse me," she said to the man in front of her as she left her place in line.

An hour or so later, Fredrika slowly pushed open the restroom door and stepped back into the room. She was quite surprised to find the guard standing right outside the door!

"Passport, please," he said, his hand extended palm up.

"Why, of course," replied Fredrika as she handed him the small blue booklet. Out of the corners of her eyes she saw that the police were still standing on either side of the exit door.

Slowly, the guard thumbed through the pages of Fredrika's passport. Suddenly, his eyes narrowed.

The next thing Fredrika knew, she was surrounded by police, and her wrists were in handcuffs. Quickly, the police escorted her out the back door.

Obviously, the guard believed Fredrika's passport was fake! Look at the tell-tale page below and see if you can guess why.

→ *WARNING* -- ANY CHANGE TO THE FACTS BELOW IS NOT ALLOWED.

NAME	
FREDRIKA FORSYTHE	

BIRTHDATE	PLACE OF BIRTH
SEPT. 32, 1958	HONOLULU, OREGON

HEIGHT	HAIR	EYES
5 FEET 7 INCHES	BROWN	GREEN

WIFE OR HUSBAND	DATE
X X X	FEBRUARY 30, 1988

CHILDREN	PASSPORT RENEWAL
X X X	

SIGNATURE
Fredrika Forsythe

→ *IMPORTANT:* UNLESS OTHER RULES APPLY, THIS PASSPORT IS GOOD FOR THREE YEARS FROM ABOVE DATE. IF RENEWED, IT IS GOOD FOR FIVE YEARS FROM ABOVE DATE.

Winter Trouble

It was snowing hard in Kirkwood, and the streets were quiet. Ellen, Nils and Sarah were out walking through town. They talked about all the fun things they would do in the days ahead. They would be building snow sculptures, sledding down hillsides, drinking hot chocolate and warming up by crackling fires.

Ellen picked up some snow and formed a ball in her mittens. Then she threw it hard at Sarah. The snowball flattened out against Sarah's red wool jacket and stuck there. Sarah laughed and threw a snowball at Nils.

Nils picked up some snow, too. He looked around for something to hit. He saw a car at the end of the block. It was headed toward them. Nils couldn't resist. He lifted up his arm and aimed the snowball just where he thought the car would pass. Then he threw it – hard.

A second later, the car sped by, and the children heard a loud *thud!* Nils' snowball had landed on target! The car *screeched* to a stop, and a young man jumped out.

Nils looked at Sarah and Sarah looked at Ellen, and suddenly they all took off running! The young man started running after them. The children ran and ran, and so did the man. They ran through the snow up one side of Main Street and down the other. They couldn't lose the man.

Ellen was afraid. She didn't know what the man was going to do! He could even put them all in jail, she thought. What would her parents say to that? Ellen's hands began to sweat with fear. She wished that Nils hadn't thrown the snowball at the man's car.

Meanwhile, Nils was thinking, "I can't believe I hit him!" Nils had never hit a *moving* object before. He was still surprised he'd succeeded!

As for Sarah, she kept thinking how funny all four of them must look running up and down the same street. Nothing so exciting had ever happened in the sleepy little town.

Finally, just outside the courthouse, the man caught up with the children. "I want all three of you to follow me," the young man said. Then he lead them into the courthouse. There, he explained the problem to the town's only judge and left the children in his hands.

The judge introduced himself and shook each child's hand. Suddenly, he said, "I know who threw the snowball – it was Ellen!" Now, Ellen looked really worried.

But Nils spoke right up, "No, your Honor, *I* threw the ball. I'm the one you should punish."

The judge apologized to Ellen. Then he said, "I don't believe punishment is called for in this case . . . That is, as long as all of you promise never to throw snowballs at cars again."

Of course, the children promised they wouldn't. And for as long as they lived in Kirkwood, they didn't!

Why did the judge think Ellen had thrown the snowball?

Hooper For Hire #1

Henry Hooper, a private detective, has been watching Jimmy's Flower Shop all afternoon. He knows something's not right. Look at the pictures below. See if you can guess why Hooper is suspicious.

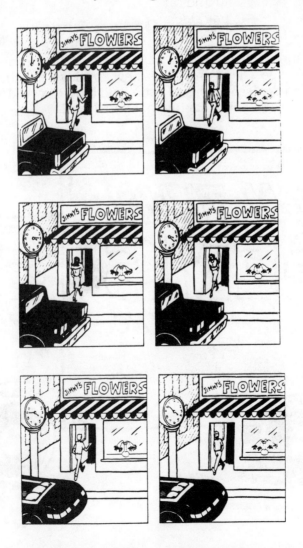

Sidetracks #2

Who or what made *these* tracks?
Hint: They were made in sand.

The Gems Of Von Juwel

It was nine o'clock at night at the close of the International Gem Show in Chicago. Claus and Hans, new employees of the famous German gem dealer Von Juwel, were still hard at work! They were beginning to regret ever having met Von Juwel.

Claus pulled the van up to the loading dock, and Hans opened the back doors. Together they piled up the boxes containing their boss's gems – jewels that could fetch as much as $1,000,000 in the United States!

Next, they would drive to O'Hare Airport, where the gems would be flown back to Germany. Then they could take it easy and spend the rest of the weekend sightseeing.

The men closed the doors and jumped in the van with Claus behind the wheel. Soon they were speeding along a dark street that ran under elevated-train tracks. Claus yawned. Suddenly, Hans yelled, "Stop!" Claus opened his eyes and saw a truck blocking the road in front of them. The driver had jumped out and was lifting the hood.

Quickly, Claus stepped on the brakes and screeched to a stop. "For Pete's sake, we're never going to make it to the airport on time!" Claus growled. Then he beeped his horn. The truck driver held his hand up at them from under the hood, then quickly stepped aside and let the hood drop shut with a *clap*. Finally, he jumped back into the truck and drove it away.

Claus stepped on the gas and continued along the road under the tracks. Hans looked out the window at the train-track beams rushing by. "Let's stop for a hot dog on our way back from the airport," he said. "I'm hungry."

Just then, Claus and Hans heard a loud *flapping* noise from outside their van. They were barely two blocks away from the gem show. "A flat!" Claus said with disgust.

He pulled the van over to the side of the road. The two men jumped out and examined their right rear tire. It was as flat as a pancake.

"You stay here," Claus said to Hans. "I'm going to look for help." Claus headed back to the gem show on foot, and Hans climbed back into the van. His stomach growled and he began to see juicy hot dogs dancing before his eyes.

Suddenly, a garbage truck pulled up on the other side of the street. It began making all sorts of grinding and wheezing noises. At about the same time, a beautiful young woman appeared, knocking on Hans' window. He rolled it down, and the woman explained that she was lost. She had to shout over the clatter of the garbage truck. Soon she began to cry. She told Hans that she'd just run away from her boyfriend over an argument. It seemed to Hans that she wanted to tell him her whole life story. In the end, it turned out that she was looking for a bus stop only a few blocks away. Even Hans, a foreign traveler, knew where the bus stop was. He was happy that he could direct the young woman to it. She thanked him and went on her way. The garbage truck moved further down the street.

Finally, Claus returned in a tow truck driven by another man. The driver helped the men change their tire, and Claus paid him for his work.

Back on the road again, they arrived at O'Hare without any further mishap and in plenty of time to spare. However, when they opened their van, they found it completely bare!

This crime took place at two locations. How many criminals were stationed at each spot? What role did each criminal play in the crime?

Sidetracks #3

If you can guess what made these tracks, you may be the world's next Sherlock Holmes!

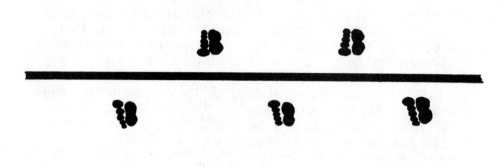

The Case Of The Almost-Great Bank Robbery

The downtown bank's alarm went off Saturday at 5:43 P.M. Four police officers were on the scene at 5:48. The bank, of course, wasn't open for business. And most of the nearby shops had closed promptly at 5:00. The only signs – and sounds – of weekend activity came from the lot next door to the bank. There, a building was going up. A few workers were on the site, walking around the wood planks framing the second story.

The officers moved swiftly. Jumping from their police cars, they slammed their doors, grabbed their guns and circled the bank. Two men, in different spots, appeared to be fleeing the scene. Two officers stopped the men and took them aside for questioning. The other two officers – one man and one woman – went inside the bank to look around.

Inside the bank vault, the officers had the surprise of their lives. Smack dab in the middle of the concrete floor was a perfectly round hole.

They lowered themselves into the hole and found a tunnel. At their feet lay a drill with diamond-tipped teeth – teeth hard enough to cut through steel. Next to the drill was a flashlight and two sandwich wrappers. Along the floor of the tunnel were footprints. The officers determined they were made by one person or more who wore size ten shoes.

The officers followed the footprints to an underground city drainage ditch. They looked around and spotted the underside of a manhole cover, which led to the noisy street overhead. "A-ha," said the male officer. "So that's how they got down here."

The female officer looked back through the tunnel leading to the bank. "It must have taken them weeks to do all this digging!" she said.

"And the racket from the building going on next door would have covered up the noise of their drilling!" said the first officer. "Very clever!"

The two officers crawled out through the manhole and joined their comrades back up on the street.

Both men being held claimed innocence. However, one of them was indeed involved in the attempted bank robbery. His partners in crime were luckier. They had managed to escape – at least for the time being!

The officers continued their questioning and taking notes. Soon they'd gathered the following information.

As chance would have it, both men wore size ten shoes. Both men were covered with dirt. (Both claimed to be construction workers and dirty from an honest day's work!) Both had very rough hands, which is what one would expect from weeks of drilling.

See if you can help the officers "get their man." Look at the pictures of the suspects. See if you can find one clue that hints at which man spent weeks digging a tunnel.

Fingerprint Clues

Why can fingerprints be used as clues? Everyone has different fingerprints. Make sets of fingerprints of yourself and of your friends. Compare the sets of prints. Do any match?

To make a set of fingerprints, you will need some white paper and an inkpad. Draw ten squares on the paper. Label the squares for each finger and each hand. Slowly roll each finger on the inkpad then roll the finger in one of the squares. Don't press too hard on the white paper. You don't want the ink to smudge. Now get a magnifying glass and study the different designs in each fingerprint.

Detectives always search for fingerprints at the scene of a crime.

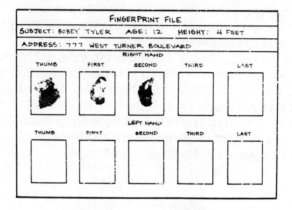

Distant Clues

Pretend that you are in a helicopter flying over a beach city. You are looking for Highway Harry, the notorious highway sign thief. You know that Highway Harry has just stolen a stop sign. Look at the picture below. They might look funny at first, but that is because they are drawn from the point of view of the helicopter. So you are looking *down* at the picture. Label each object and find Highway Harry carrying the stop sign.

Hooper For Hire #2

It was a dark, cold, moonless night. The two-story warehouse stood alone in the middle of an empty lot. Quietly, Henry Hooper tiptoed up to a window at the back and slipped inside. Brushing dust off his coat, he pulled a flashlight from his pocket and turned it on. Just as he suspected, there in the beam of the light stood his client's stolen black sports car.

The car was parked next to several buckets of light blue paint. "Looks like I found it just in time – before it got repainted and resold!" thought Hooper, smiling to himself.

Suddenly, Hooper heard a noise. Swiftly, someone grabbed him from behind and wrapped a blindfold over his eyes. "We don't like snoops around here," growled a low male voice.

The next thing Hooper knew, he was alone in a room upstairs. Still blindfolded, he lay on a cot next to a window that was tightly locked. His hands and his feet were tied.

As the hours slowly passed in silence, Hooper planned his escape and capture of the car thieves.

Finally, Hooper heard the door open and someone shuffle into the room. "Good morning, friend," said Hooper cheerfully, for he knew he'd have the thieves in jail by sundown!

How did Hooper know that it was morning? Remember that he was blindfolded, so he couldn't have seen the sun rising through the window. Also, the hours passed in silence, so he didn't hear the chiming of a church tower clock.

Sidetracks #4

Here are some strange-looking tracks. Guess what made them!

The Case Of Missing Directions

Adam and Andrea, two plainclothes detectives, drove an unmarked patrol car. One day, while they were driving their patrol car, a message came over their car radio. "Robbery suspect leaving scene of crime. Last *nese* headed *tews* on Elm *testre.*"

Adam, who was driving, stepped on the gas. "Where are you going?" asked Andrea.

"I'm going to find the robbery suspect," said Adam.

"Did you understand the radio message?" asked Andrea.

"No. I thought you did," said Adam.

"I didn't understand either. Maybe I should ask the operator to repeat the message." said Andrea as she called into the station.

"This is Detective Andrea. Could you repeat the message?" Andrea asked.

They didn't hear anything but static on the radio. Finally, the police radio person's voice was heard on the radio. The radio person said, "*Scpuset* now headed *seat* on *Alppe* Drive. Please follow."

Adam turned the car around again and stepped on the gas.

As they drove past where they had just been, Andrea asked, "Where are you going now?"

"I don't know. I didn't understand the directions. Did you?" asked Adam.

Andrea was getting mad. She could see that they were getting nowhere fast. She called the station again for directions.

They heard the radio operator say, "Head *ornth,* on Highway 101. Make *ftel* turn, continue on until you come to a *kofr* in the road. We think suspect is driving to his house in *SOOGE* Hollow. Over and out." The radio went dead.

Adam and Andrea looked at each other. They shook their heads. They still couldn't understand the directions. So they kept driving in circles.

Help Adam and Andrea follow the suspect. The words in *italics* in the story are misspelled. Unscramble the letters and write them on a piece of paper.

6'6"
6'0"
5'9" —
5'6"
5'0"
4'6"

6'3" —

5'6" —

SUSPECT #1   SUSPECT #2   SUSPECT #3

Line-Up

All three of the above men are suspects in the theft of Henrietta Farnsworth's diamond brooch. All three knew that Henrietta was out of town on the evening of November 3. All three were seen at different times outside Henrietta's mansion that evening. All three had reason to write "Now we're even" on Henrietta's front door. However, only one suspect is guilty.

The message, written about six feet from the ground, was the only clue the police had to go on.

Read the descriptions of each of the suspects below. Then look at the line-up. Decide who you think stole Mrs. Farnsworth's brooch.

Suspect 1: Gardener. Has worked for Mrs. Farnsworth for 20 years without a single paid vacation. He was heard to mutter, "Mrs. Farnsworth *owes* me! And I think I know a way she can pay me back!" His voice was said to have contained a great deal of bitterness as he uttered these words.

Suspect 2: Ex-fiance of Mrs. Farnsworth, a widower for the last nine years. Mrs. Farnsworth broke the engagement when she discovered that the suspect wanted to marry her only for her money. He was said to be quite upset over this development.

Suspect 3: Mrs. Farnsworth's poor cousin, an unemployed loafer whom Henrietta helped for many years, recently was "cut off" by Henrietta, who thought it was high time her cousin start looking for work. The suspect became outraged and complained widely that Henrietta had broken her promise to buy him a new car.

Another Whodunit For Super Super Sleuths!

Read the last "Whodunit." Now suppose that *just one of the Cheats brothers is a liar who never tells the truth.* Now which one of the brothers do you think is guilty of taking Mr. Larousse's fountain pen?

Mystery On Moore Street

The mystery on Moore Street started the same day that eight-year-old Alison Huyke decided to start her own detective agency. Alison had just finished hanging up her detective sign when her first customers arrived – Curious Curtis and Nosy Natalie.

"Are you open for business, Alison?" asked Curious Curtis.

"I sure am," replied Alison, point to her sign. The sign read, "Huycke's Detective Agency. 10¢ a mystery."

"Well we have a mystery for you to solve," said Nosy Natalie. "You know that new kid who moved in down the street?"

"I haven't met him yet," said Alison.

"Well we have, and he's very confusing," said Curious Curtis.

"Confusing?"

"Yes. Here's what happened. I went over and introduced myself to him. I found out that his name is Vic. I asked him if he wanted to play baseball tomorrow at three. He said he would love to play baseball," said Curious Curtis.

"So what's the big mystery?" asked Alison.

"Well, I asked him to go to the movies tomorrow at three," said Nosy Natalie. "How can he be in two places at once?"

"Maybe he has a twin brother," said Alison.

"No. He said he didn't have any brothers or sisters," said Curious Curtis.

"Well, I think I can find out if he is a twin or not," said Alison. "I'll have an answer for you in half an hour."

Alison stuffed three licorice sticks in her pocket, then she set off to meet the new kid, Vic. When she arrived at Vic's house, she looked around. She didn't see anyone, so she knocked on the door. Vic answered the door. She introduced herself and offered Vic a licorice stick.

"Thanks. I love licorice," said Vic as he ate the licorice.

"Have another piece," offered Alison, "Do you have any brothers or sisters?"

"No, I'm an only child. That's why we moved here so I could get to know other kids. Already, I've met you, Curious Curtis and Nosy Natalie," said Vic chewing his second piece of black licorice.

"Oh, I forgot I wanted to show you my marble collection. I'll just run home and get it, okay?" said Alison.

"Great," said Vic.

Alison ran home. She grabbed her marble collection and ran back to Vic's house. When she returned, she looked around for Vic but he was gone. So she knocked on the door again. Vic answered the door – at least the boy *looked* like Vic. Alison stared at his pearly white toothed smile.

When the boy who looked exactly like Vic smiled, Alison knew that he wasn't Vic. Vic had lied when he said he didn't have any brothers or sisters. He had an identical twin.

"You have an identical twin named Vic, don't you?" said Alison.

"Yes. My name is Dick. We just wanted to play a little joke on all the new kids we meet. How did you know?" asked Dick.

How did Alison know that Vic had an identical twin?

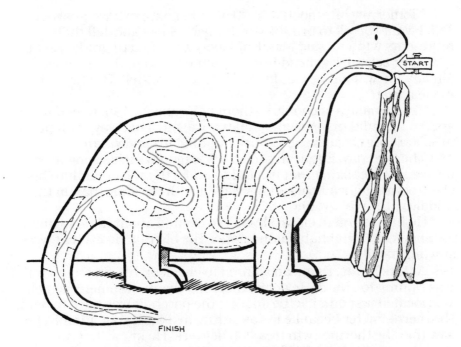

Escape From The Dinosaur

Professor Bones, the dinosaur detective, is in big trouble. While out searching for fossils, he wandered into a huge, dark cave. But it wasn't a cave – it was the open mouth of a dinosaur! Before Professor Bones could escape from the dinosaur's mouth, the dinosaur swallowed him.

Help Professor Bones escape from the dinosaur by tracing a path with your finger through the dinosaur's body to his tail.

The Case Of The Missing Snowman

Egghead Magoo thought he was the smartest boy in the world. He could spell more words and do longer math problems than anyone else in his class. But the day his snowman disappeared, Egghead learned that he wasn't the smartest boy in the world after all. Here's what happened.

"Tomorrow afternoon at 3:00, we are going to have Show-and-Tell. I want you all to bring something for Show-and-Tell that represents winter," said Mrs. Engleberry, the fourth grade teacher.

After school, Egghead hurried home through the snow. He already knew what he would take to Show-and-Tell. But he had to make it first.

"I will make a snowman," thought Egghead, "Snowmen mean winter. I'll build my snowman on my wagon. That way I can pull it to school." Egghead went to work building his snowman.

The next day, Egghead pulled his wagon with his snowman on it to school. Realizing that he couldn't take the snowman into his classroom, Egghead parked his wagon with the snowman in the middle of the playground.

He hurried off to class. He was so excited about his snowman for Show-and-Tell that he didn't notice the big rain drops that were starting to fall.

At lunchtime, Egghead wanted to check on his snowman but it was raining too hard. He decided to read the thermometer which was located just outside the door on the porch. It was hard to read the thermometer because it was sitting in a dark spot. Finally, he saw that the thermometer read 30 degrees. He knew that 30 degrees was cold enough for water to freeze. So he figured the rain wouldn't hurt his snowman; in fact, the freezing rain would freeze the snow. So he decided not to go out until it was time for Show-and-Tell.

Finally, it was 3:00, time for Show-and-Tell. Egghead raised his hand.

"Could I be excused to go get my Show-and-Tell?" asked Egghead.

"Yes, but come right back," said Mrs. Engleberry.

Egghead raced through the rain to the playground to get his snowman. But when he got there he found that his snowman had disappeared. His wagon was where he had left it. But the snowman was gone.

Egghead raced back to class. He was very upset.

"My snowman is missing," cried Egghead.

"Yes, but it's been raining. That's why it melted," said Mrs. Engleberry.

"It couldn't melt," said Egghead. "I read the thermometer on the porch at noon. It read 30 degrees. That is cold enough to freeze snow and water. No, someone must have stolen my snowman," said Egghead.

"Well, if the temperature was higher than 30 degrees then the rain could have melted your snowman, right?" asked Mrs. Engleberry.

"Yes," said Egghead.

"You said that you looked at the thermometer on the porch. If that thermometer read 30 degrees then it was warmer out on the open playground. So, your snowman melted," said Mrs. Engleberry.

After several minutes, Egghead realized that his snowman wasn't missing. It really had melted. He also realized that he wasn't the smartest boy in the world.

How did Mrs. Engleberry know that it was warmer on the open playground?

Slippery Louie's Note

Slippery Louie has escaped from prison again. The police think he is in another country. The only clue to Slippery Louie's whereabouts is the note below.

Help the police figure out which country Slippery Louie is hiding in. Do this on a piece of paper. Add and subtract the letters in the names of the things shown in the picture puzzle. Then write the letters in the boxes. Keep the letters in order. The letters are your clues.

The Case Of The Missing Baseball Card

Joan Swanson liked to do two things, solve mysteries and collect baseball cards. By the time she was 12 years old, she had solved 99 mysteries and collected 100 valuable baseball cards. They day she solved her hundredth mystery was the day her favorite baseball card was stolen. Here's what happened.

One day, Joan was sorting her baseball cards when the doorbell rang. It was her friend Louise Radar and a boy whom Joan didn't know.

"Hi, Joan. This is my cousin Petey Radar," said Louise.

"Nice to meet you," said Joan. "Come on in the living room. I'm just sorting my baseball card collection."

"I collect baseball cards too," said Petey as the three kids walked into the living room.

"We both brought our card collections," answered Louise. "Maybe we can do a little trading."

"Okay," said Joan.

The three kids lined up their cards. Then they compared cards. Joan traded her Baltimore Oriole card of catcher Terry Kennedy for Petey's Milwaukee Brewer's card of infielder Paul Molitor. Louise didn't have any cards that Joan or Petey wanted. Joan picked up her cards and set them on the desk near the open window. Her favorite card, a Willie Mays baseball card, sat on the top of the deck.

"Mom just made some chocolate chip cookies. Want some?" asked Joan.

"Sure," said Petey and Louise together.

"I wish you would trade me your Willie Mays card," said Petey.

"Forget it, Petey. She wouldn't trade her Willie Mays card for the whole Dodger line-up," said Louise.

"Right. It's my favorite card. Besides it's a really rare baseball card," said Joan.

"Come on, let's get some cookies," said Joan. Joan and Louise started towards the kitchen. Petey stayed in the living room a few minutes longer.

After several seconds, Petey joined them in the kitchen. They helped themselves to cookies.

"These are great," said Louise as she stuffed two cookies into her mouth.

"Chocolate chip is my favorite," said Petey helping himself to a few more cookies.

Suddenly, Louise got up and started out of the kitchen.

"Where are you going? Don't you want some more cookies?" asked Joan.

"I'll be right back. I just want to check on the bikes. We left them out in front," said Louise.

"They'll be okay. No one steals in this neighborhood. Everyone knows I'm a junior detective," laughed Joan.

"I know. I'll just check," said Louise.

While Louise was gone, Petey and Joan started talking about movies. Joan heard Louise open and close the front door.

"I don't know why she worries about that old bike of hers," said Joan. "She would have to pay someone to take it."

After several seconds, Louise joined Joan and Petey in the kitchen. When the kids couldn't eat any more cookies, they decided to return to the living room.

"Want to play cards or some game?" asked Joan.

"No. We have to get going. My parents are going to pick me up at 5:00," said Petey.

"Thanks for the cookies," said Louise.

Just as the kids were leaving, Joan noticed that her Willie Mays card was gone.

"Hey, wait a minute. My Willie Mays card is gone," said Joan. No one has been in here except you two. So one of you has it."

Petey and Louise looked at each other. Finally, Petey said, "We didn't steal it. When I was straightening up my pile of cards, I saw your card fall on the floor. I guess the wind blew it off your pile."

"Yeah, then where is it?" asked Joan.

"I put it back on the desk near the lamp," said Petey.

Joan looked near the lamp. The card was not there.

"It was there a little while ago," said Petey.

"Did you see it, Louise?" asked Joan.

Louise looked uncomfortable.

"I saw it when I passed the living room on my way to check my bike. The wind must have blown it off the desk again. So I put it in the blue book on the desk. You'll find it between pages 55 and 56," said Louise, happy to have solved the mystery.

When Joan looked there was no baseball card. Joan stared at the book for several seconds. Then she stared at Louise and Petey. She knew who had taken her baseball card.

Who stole the baseball card? How did Joan know who stole the card?

Bosco The Bloodhound

Recently, a group of mystery writers attended a convention. The mystery writers came from countries all around the world. On the first day of the meeting, everyone wore a costume which represented his or her country. It was a very colorful meeting.

The convention lasted a week. On the last day, everyone started to pack their clothes to go home. But they soon discovered that some of their clothes were missing. No one knew what to do. Finally, Sir Barry Benton suggested that they send Bosco the Bloodhound in search of the missing clothes.

Bosco the Bloodhound searched and searched. Finally, he found the missing clothes in the laundry. The maid had thought she was suppose to wash everything. It was an honest mistake so no one was angry. Bosco the Bloodhound had found the articles of clothing but he didn't know whom each article of clothing belonged to.

Help Bosco the Bloodhound return the missing clothing to the right owner. The names of the owners are listed in the left-hand column. On a piece of paper write the letter for clothing that goes with the number of the person.

1. Ian of Scotland	a. sombrero
2. Caesar of ancient Rome	b. grass skirt
3. Marta of Mexico	c. bobby socks
4. Running Bear, an American Indian	d. toga
5. Colleen of Ireland	e. wooden shoes
6. Shirley of the United States	f. fur parka
7. Suki of Japan	g. moccasins
8. Gretel of Holland	h. kilts
9. Moki the Eskimo	i. kimono
10. Pele of Hawaii	j. green shamrock skirt
11. Gunther of Germany	k. liederhosen

The Chocolate Chip Cookie Caper

One summer day, Grandma Jane decided to wash her kitchen floor. The floor had gotten dirty earlier when she had made chocolate chip cookies. "Oh well, the cookie jar is full now and I have a few left over for my neighbor," said Grandma Jane to herself. After washing the floor, Grandma Jane decided to take her neighbor the plate of extra cookies while the floor dried. She closed the kitchen window and locked the back door. On the way to the neighbor's, she passed Tony the gardener. Tony was planting seeds in the flower bed. Then she passed three-year-old Buddy Sullivan playing in his plastic swimming pool. Grandma Jane gave both Tony and Buddy a chocolate chip cookie.

Later when Grandma Jane returned home, she found that someone had been in her kitchen. Look at the picture below of Grandma Jane's kitchen. The clues in the story and the clues in the picture will help you solve the mystery. Answer the following questions:

1. How did the thief enter the kitchen?
2. What did the thief steal?
3. Who was the thief?
4. How do you know who the thief was?

Sidetracks #5

A thief is on the loose! Police have roped off a full city block at all four corners. Officers are searching each and every building. Here are the thief's footprints – on this page and the next.
Can you guess where he is and what he is doing?

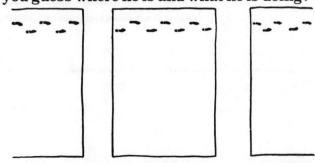

39

The Camera Caper

You are a detective. Your police captain has just assigned you to investigate a robbery at Carson's Camera Shop.

You arrive at Carson's Camera Shop. The first thing you see is the broken glass door of the shop. You notice the broken glass on the sidewalk. You step over the glass and enter the shop. You introduce yourself to Mr. Carson, the owner of the store. You ask Mr. Carson to tell you what happened.

According to Mr. Carson, the robber entered the store about 11 p.m. The robber got into the store by breaking the glass door and unlocking the inside lock. Twelve expensive cameras were stolen. Mr. Carson explains that the thief must have been in the shop before because he only took expensive cameras.

You ask Mr. Carson where he was during the robbery. He explains that after closing the store for the night, he had decided to take a nap in the back room. He was asleep when the robbery happened. He states that he heard the glass break but by the time he got to the front of the store the thief was gone.

You then ask Mr. Carson if the cameras were insured. He nods. Then, he explains how he will buy new cameras with the insurance money. He hopes you can catch the robber.

You smile. You know that Mr. Carson is the robber. You suggest that Mr. Carson take a little ride with you to the police station.

How do you know that Mr. Carson is the robber? Why would Mr. Carson steal his own cameras?

The Great Excuse

One day, Joey Johnson was late for dinner. His father was very angry.

"You are two hours late. Where have you been, Joey?" said Mr. Johnson. "Your mother and I have been very worried about you."

"I can explain," said Joey.

"You'd better have a good excuse," said Mr. Johnson.

"I was locked in a room," said Joey.

"What?" said Mr. Johnson.

"On the way home from school, two big bullies grabbed me. They forced me to go into the old abandoned house on River Street. They dragged me into a room and locked the door. Then they left," said Joey.

"How terrible," said Joey's mother.

"It was. There weren't any windows in the room. I didn't know what to do," said Joey.

"So how did you escape?" asked Mr. Johnson.

"I took the hinges off the door. It was hard to get those hinges off. Then I ran straight home," said Joey.

"That was quick thinking, Joey," said Mr. Johnson, who was frowning. "Just tell me one thing. Did the door open into the room or did it swing out of the room?"

Joey thought for a moment then said, "The door opened out. That's what made it so hard to get the hinges off."

"That's a great excuse, Joey. There's just one problem with your excuse; it's not the truth," said Mr. Johnson. "You didn't escape from that room because you were never in that room. Now where were you?"

"I was playing baseball with Timmy. I'm sorry. I forgot about the time," said Joey sheepishly.

"Next time, don't be late and no more excuses," said Mr. Johnson.

How did Mr. Johnson know that Joey's excuse was a fib?

Look Out Mountain Hideout

Two dangerous bank robbers named Hank and Blank liked to rob banks. After robbing a bank they would ride to their hideout on Look Out Mountain. No one had ever been able to find them because their hideout was hidden so well. Texas Rangers, local sheriffs and bounty hunters had all tried to find Hank and Blank's hideout. But every time someone tried to follow Hank and Blank there, they got lost.

The bank is offering a big reward for the capture of Hank and Blank. Try to find their hideout and win the big reward.

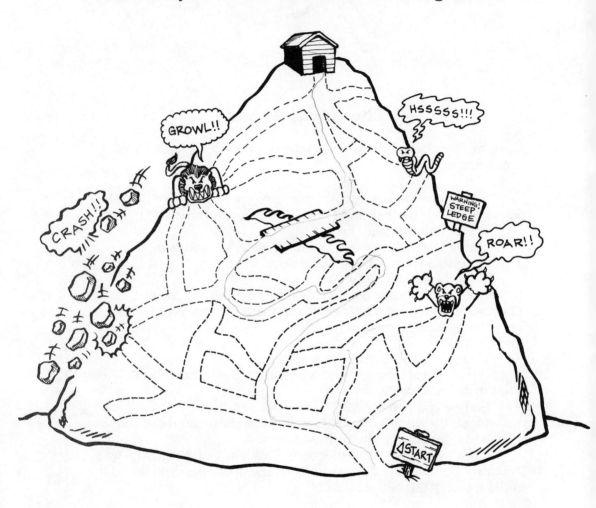

The Farmer's Problem

This often-told mystery has an interesting solution. Read the facts then try to solve the mystery.

A farmer had a wolf, a lamb and a sack of grass. He was taking the wolf, the lamb and the sack of grass to his farm. On the way to his farm, he had to cross a wide river. The river wasn't very deep so the farmer could carry the lamb, the wolf and the sack of grass across the river. He knew that he could only carry one thing at a time. This was a problem. The farmer knew that if he left the lamb with the wolf while he carried the sack of grass across, the wolf would eat the lamb. If he left the lamb with the grass while he carried the wolf across, the lamb would eat the grass.

How did the farmer solve his problem?

MYSTERY SOLUTIONS

Page 3 Mysterious Treasure
Solution: diamond ring, chain, goblet, spyglass, two coins, bottle, pirate pistol, earring and bowl.

Page 4 A Whodunit For Super Sleuths
Solution: The opposite of each man's answer is as follows. Huey: I didn't take it. Duey: Huey didn't take it. Louey: It was Huey or Duey. If all three statements are true, only Duey could have taken Mr. Larousse's gold fountain pen.

Page 5 Mystery Of The Unlabeled Bottles
Solution: The poison was arsenic.

Page 6 Case Of The Missing Fathers
Solution: The following figures belong together: A and K, B and L, C and H, D and I, E and G, F and J.

Page 7 Coin Puzzle Mystery
Solution: Snidely Swipe blew the coin out of the plate.

Page 7 Coffee Caper
Solution: He left the coffee in its can. The coffee was not liquid when he hid the sugar cube.

Page 8 Tricky Clue
Solution: Diamonds Malone was hiding at the North Pole. He wrote in his note that every side of his square house faced south. Super Sleuth Sam knew that the only place on earth where each side of the house would face south was the North Pole.

Page 8 Puzzler
Solution: If Julia had discovered a liquid that could dissolve any substance, then the bottle containing the liquid would have also dissolved.

Page 9 Mysterious Dinosaur Drawings
Solution: Dinosaurs roamed the earth before human beings existed.

Page 9 You Be The Eyewitness
Solution: Your description should include the same details as written in book – tall, thin man with blonde hair and blue eyes. He wore old blue jeans patched at the knee and a sports shirt with an alligator on it. He had a black tennis shoe on his right foot and a white tennis shoe on his left foot. He carried a pillow in his left hand and a candlestick in his right hand. He was about 21 years old.

Page 10 Vanished
Solution One: If the hurricane was able to take away much of Puerto Bello's beach, it might cause the disappearance of a small island. But since Jose's favorite island was so close to another island, the hurricane would have caused both to disappear.

Solution Two:: There might have been so many tourists taking so many seashells (and the sand they found them in) that little by little they ended up taking the entire island. However, this sort of thing happens only in cartoons.

Solution Three: As the story points out, Rico Rivera used a great deal of sand in his cement factory – tons of it at a time. It had been many years since Jose had seen his favorite island. During this time, Rico Rivera could easily have used up all of the island's fine white sand and caused its disappearance.

Page 11 Tell-Tale Clock
Solution: Widow Miller said that she saw Jimmy at 11:05. Jimmy Sticky-Fingers and Bob the Barber both said that Jimmy was in the barber shop at 11:05. Both Jimmy and Bob had seen the clock reflected in the mirror. Minute Marty knew that if the reflection of the clock in the mirror read 11:05, the true time would have been 12:55. (Try holding a watch to a mirror. Read the time on your watch. Now look at the watch in the mirror. What time is it?)

Page 12 **Cherry Pie Connection**
Solution: Sneaky Pete's message reads: "The boys and I'll bust you out at sundown. Be Ready!"

Page 13 **Picture Word Clues**
Solution: Charley saw a bear.

Page 14 **Study In Orange**
Solution: Though carrots are very good for the body, one can eat too many! After several weeks of eating more than the daily requirement, one's skin can become orangish in color. Dr. Dodd probably advised Ramona to cut back on the amount of carrots she was eating every day.

Page 15 **Carmelita Cooke And The Seven Crooks**
Solutions (here, solutions are mistakes you find in the story): 1. Chicago sits on Lake Michigan, not Lake Superior. 2. Carmelita's headquarters was a one-room studio apartment, but she met her men behind closed doors in her living room. 3. If Carmelita's headquarters overlooks the lake from the Chicago shoreline, she could only see the sun rise, not set. (Chicago is on the west side of Lake Michigan.) 4. If the sun *could* be seen setting, it would be setting over a like, not an ocean. 5. If the maid had just cleared the luncheon dishes, it would have been too early for the sun to set. 6. If indeed Thursday was December 30, Sunday would have been January 2. 7. Only six of the seven men are accounted for in the break-in plans and in the break-in itself. 8. It was Fast Eddy, not Lefty, who was assigned to take the Picasso. 9. It would have been more accurate to say, "it took more than *two* times their number to shut their business down."

Page 16 **The Case Of The Secret Markings**
Solution: Find "Beaufield" hidden in the king's robe and his necklace. Find "Harlin" hidden in the king's beard and his crown.

Page 17 **Sidetracks #1**
Solution: An elephant learning how to ride a motorcycle and a kangaroo on a pogo stick – of course!

Page 17 **Faking It**
Solution: 1. The word two shouldn't be one a one dollar bill. 2. Instead of United States of America, it says, "Unified."

Page 18 **Curtain Call At Lacy's**
Solution: Gladys' bracelet!

Page 19 **Mixed-Up Wanted Posters**
Solution: Posters one and five

Page 19 **The Hunt Is On!**
Solution: The coded message found in Fraser Caulfield's hotel room reads: "Call George at once: (919) 555-4514."

Page 20 **The July Meeting Of The Mayfield Women's Mystery Club**
Solution: The member who "snuck" into Mabel's guestroom is the one wearing a zebra-print dress. Note the button that got caught in the drawer.

Page 21 **Trapped!**
Solution: No official document would ever contain the wrong city in a state. Is Honolulu in Oregon?

Page 22 **Winter Trouble**
Solution: Ellen's hands were wet from sweat. The judge must have thought they were wet from holding – and throwing – the snowball.

Page 23 **Hooper For Hire #1**
Solution: First of all, no flowers are displayed in the windows. Second, none of Jimmy's customers stays long or buys any flowers. It is obvious that the shop is conducting business far more sinister than selling flowers!

Page 24 **Sidetracks #2**
Solution: Anyone can see that these tracks were made by a blind man in a wheelchair being pushed by a woman with one peg leg!

Page 25 **The Gems Of Von Juwel**
Solution: It took at least six criminals to pull off the theft of Von Juwel's gems. At the first location, one person drove the truck and blocked the road. Another person punctured the tire on the van without being caught. At the second location, one person had to drive the garbage truck – the noise prevented the people inside the van from hearing the back doors being opened. Another person had to talk to the man in the can to distract him while the theft was taking place – another precaution. The fifth person had to perform the theft, and the sixth had to drive the get-away car.

Page 26 **Sidetracks #3**
Solution: Obviously, these are the footprints of a woman who's taken off her shoes and is pushing a wheelbarrow on her tiptoes. No doubt the wheelbarrow contains stolen goods. Why else would she not want to make any noise?

Page 26 **The Case Of The Almost Great Bank Robbery**
Solution: Digging a tunnel requires that one spend a great deal of time on one's knees. This fact may well account for the holes in one of the men's jeans.

Page 28 **Elevator Mystery**
Solution: He could only reach the fourth floor button in the elevator. He was too short to reach the button for the fourteenth floor.

Page 28 **Fingerprint Clues**
Solution: none.

Page 28 **Distant Clues**

Page 29 **Sidetracks #4**
Solution: Of course, these are tracks made by a trained French poodle on stilts, too afraid to move!

Page 29 **Hooper For Hire #2**
Solution: The only explanation is that Hooper felt the heat of the sun through the window.

Page 30 **The Case Of Missing Directions**
Solution: nese . . . seen, tews . . . west, testre . . . street, scpuset . . . suspect, seat . . . east, alppe . . . apple, ornth . . . north, ftel . . . left, koft . . . fork, sooge . . . goose.

Page 31 **Another Whodunit For Super Super Sleuths**
Solution: If only one man is lying, two must be telling the truth. The only two who can be telling the truth are the two whose answers agree. Thus, in this whodunit, Huey is the thief, Louey is the liar and Duey is completely innocent!

Page 31 **Line-Up**
Solution: It is a known fact that when people write on a surface while standing they tend to write at eye level. If one of the three men is guilty, then it is most likely Mrs. Farnsworth's poor cousin. He stands 6'3 which would put his eyes at about six feet from the ground. The gardener and the ex-fiancee would have left messages lower than six feet.

Page 32 **Mystery On Moore Street**
Solution: Alison gave Vic some black licorice. He ate two pieces. When you eat black licorice, your tongue and teeth have black licorice stains. the boy who came to the door the second time looked exactly like Vic but his teeth were very white. He hadn't eaten any licorice. Alison knew that Vic's teeth had licorice stains, but the boy who answered the second time didn't. The second boy looked exactly like Vic – he was Vic's identical twin. Vic had lied when he said he was an only child.

Page 33 Escape From The Dinosaur

Page 34 The Case Of The Missing Snowman
Solution: Mrs. Engleberry knew that the thermometer on the porch was located in a shady spot. It is always a few degrees cooler in the shade. The snowman was not sitting in the shade so the temperature of air near the snowman would have been a few degrees higher than 30. When the temperature rises above 30 degrees, water will not freeze. Therefore, the snowman melted.

Page 35 Slippery Louie's Note
Solution: Canada

Page 36 Case Of The Missing Baseball Card
Solution: Louise stole the baseball card. Joan knew that Louise stole the baseball card because Louise said that she placed the card in the book between the pages 55 and 56. In a book page 56 is printed on the back of page 55.

Page 37 Chocolate Cookie Caper
Solution: The thief entered the kitchen through the window. In the picture the window is open. Grandma Jane had closed the window before going to the neighbor's. There are also dirty handprints on the window ledge. The thief stole the chocolate chip cookies. Grandma Jane had filled the cookie jar. In the picture the cookie jar is tipped over and empty. Tony the gardener stole the cookies. The only thing stolen were the cookies. Only two people knew that Grandma Jane had baked cookies that day – Tony the gardener and little Buddy Sullivan. It was not Buddy because he was too small to climb up, open and crawl through the window. Buddy was also clean. He was playing in his little swimming pool. Tony could reach up and open the window then crawl in. Tony was also dirty from working in the garden. There were dirty shoeprints and dirty handprints in the kitchen.

Page 38 Bosco The Bloodhound
Solution: These pairs go together: 1 and h, 2 and d, 3 and a, 4 and g, 5 and j, 6 and c, 7 and i, 8 and e, 9 and f, 10 and b, 11 and k.

Page 39 Sidetracks #5
Solution: The thief has just jumped from one rooftop to another!

Page 40 Camera Caper
Solution: Mr. Carson said that the robber entered the store by breaking the glass door. When you arrived at the camera store, you saw that the glass door was broken. You also saw that the broken glass was on the sidewalk outside the store. If a robber broke the glass from outside the store the glass would have fallen inside the store. The only person in the store was Mr. Carson. He stole the cameras to collect the insurance money.

Page 41 Great Excuse
Solution: Mr. Johnson knew Joey was lying when Joey said that the door opened out. If a door opens out of a room the hinges on the door would not be inside the room. If the hinges were not inside the room, Joey could not have taken the hinges off to remove the door.

Page 42 Look Out Mountain Hideout

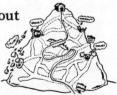

Page 43 Farmer's Problem
Solution: First, the farmer carried the lamb across the river. Then he went back and got the sack of grass across the river. When he put the sack of grass down on the other side, he picked up the lamb. He took the lamb back across the river. He put the lamb down and picked up the wolf. He carried the wolf across the river. Then he went back across the river and got the lamb again. So you see, the lamb went across the river first and last.

INDEX